Megan
the Monday
Fairy

For Tabitha Runchman

Special thanks to
Narinder Dhami

No part of this work may be reproduced, stored in a retrieval system, or transmitted in any form or by any means, electronic, mechanical, photocopying, recording, or otherwise, without written permission of the publisher. For information regarding permission, write to Rainbow Magic Limited c/o HIT Entertainment, 830 South Greenville Avenue, Allen, TX 75002-3320.

ISBN-10: 0-545-06743-X
ISBN-13: 978-0-545-06743-0

12 11 10 9 8 7 6 5 4 3 2 1   8 9 10 11 12 13/0

Printed in the U.S.A.

First Scholastic printing, August 2008

Megan
the Monday
Fairy

by Daisy Meadows

LITTLE APPLE

SCHOLASTIC INC.

New York Toronto London Auckland Sydney
Mexico City New Delhi Hong Kong Buenos Aires

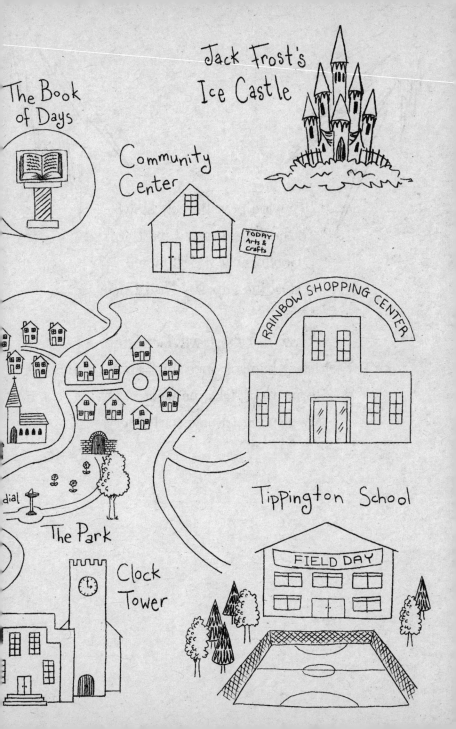

Icy wind now fiercely blow!
To the Time Tower I must go.
Goblins will all follow me
And steal the Fun Day Flags I need.

I know that there will be no fun,
For fairies or humans once the flags are gone.
Storm winds, take me where I say.
My plan for trouble starts today!

Contents

Off to Fairyland!

"I'm glad I'm staying with you during vacation," Kirsty Tate told her friend, Rachel Walker, as they came out of Fashion Fun, the accessory store on Tippington's Main Street. "And I hope these sparkly clips will look good with my new haircut!"

"I'm sure they will," Rachel said cheerfully. "They're so pretty."

"Thanks," Kirsty replied. "I wonder how the fairies are," she added, lowering her voice.

Rachel and Kirsty shared a magical secret: when they first met each other on a very special trip to Rainspell Island, they also became friends with the fairies!

"I hope Jack Frost and his goblins are behaving themselves," Rachel said.

Cold, wicked Jack Frost and his mean

goblins often caused trouble for the fairies. But the girls had helped their tiny friends outwit Jack Frost many times.

"Look, Rachel!" Kirsty said, peering into a nearby window. "This store wasn't open the last time I was here. Isn't it great?"

The store was called Dancing Days, and the window was full of dance outfits and shoes. There were white tutus,

satin ballet slippers with pink ribbons,
and sparkly tap shoes.

"I'd love to be able to tap dance," said
Rachel.

Just then the door opened and a lady
came out, followed by a girl with a long,
brown ponytail.

The girl's face lit up
when she saw Rachel.
"Hi, Rachel!" she called.
"Hi, Karen," said Rachel
with a smile. "Kirsty, this is
Karen. She's my friend
from school. And this is
her mom, Mrs. Lewis."

Karen grinned at Kirsty. "It's nice to
meet you," she said. "Rachel talks about
you all the time!"

Kirsty laughed. "Are you learning to

dance?" she asked, glancing at Karen's
blue bag.

"Yes," Karen replied. "I have tap class
at the town hall this afternoon and Mom
just bought me some new tap shoes. My
old ones were worn out."

"That's because she practices so much!"
Mrs. Lewis said, smiling. She glanced at
her watch. "We'd better hurry,
Karen."

"See you later!" Karen
called as they left.

"Maybe you could sign
up for Karen's tap
classes," Kirsty suggested
to Rachel as they
walked down the street.

"Good idea," Rachel
agreed. Then she glanced

around. "Should we walk home through the park?"

"Sure!" Kirsty replied.

The girls walked through the iron park gate and across the grass. The park was filled with colorful flowers, and in the middle was a large brass sundial shining in the light.

"The sun's bright today," Kirsty said.
Rachel nodded. Then she noticed
something that made her heart beat
faster — tiny golden sparkles were
hovering and dancing above the sundial!

"Kirsty, look at the sundial!" Rachel
gasped. "I think it's fairy magic!"

Kirsty's eyes widened. Rachel was right! And now the golden sparkles were moving. As the girls watched, the fairy dust drifted down to circle around a tiny door in the base of the sundial.

Rachel frowned. "I've seen this sundial hundreds of times, but I've never noticed

a door before," she said. Suddenly, the little door burst open and a frog hopped out. He wore a sharp red vest and a gold pocket watch. "Hello, Rachel. Hello, Kirsty," he croaked. The girls beamed at him. "You must be

from Fairyland!" Rachel guessed.

The frog nodded. "I'm Francis, the Royal Time Guard," he explained. "I'm a friend of Bertram's." The girls had met Bertram, the frog footman, during one of their fairy adventures.

"Is everything OK?" Kirsty asked.

Francis shook his head, looking sad. "The King and Queen of Fairyland need your help!" he croaked. "Will you come with me?"

"Yes, of course!" Rachel and Kirsty said together.

"Thank you, girls." Francis smiled. He reached into his pocket, pulled out some fairy dust, and threw it into the air.

9

Immediately, a dazzling rainbow, shimmering with color, began to rise from the ground.

"Follow me," said Francis, hopping onto the end of the rainbow.

Rachel and Kirsty both stepped carefully onto the rainbow with Francis.

"Now off we go!" he said with a smile. In a shower of sparkles, the rainbow whisked them off to Fairyland.

The Time Tower

In the blink of an eye, Kirsty and Rachel found themselves in Fairyland! They had transformed into fairies with glittering wings on their backs. In front of them stood the silver palace with its four pink towers, along with King Oberon and Queen Titania.

The king and queen were surrounded
by a group of fairies. Both Rachel and
Kirsty could see that they all looked very
unhappy. But why?

Francis jumped off the end of the
rainbow and bowed to the king and
queen. "Your Majesties," he announced

as the girls stepped off the rainbow, too.
"Here are our good friends, Kirsty and
Rachel!"

Queen Titania hurried forward with a
welcoming smile on her face. "It's very
good of you girls to come," she said.
"We really need your help!"

"What's wrong?" asked Rachel.

"Is it Jack Frost?" Kirsty added.

Queen Titania nodded. "Jack Frost has stolen the Fun Day Flags!" she sighed. "And now the Fun Day Fairies can't make every day fun in Fairyland and the human world."

Rachel and Kirsty glanced at the fairies. They looked miserable, and their wings drooped.

"These are our Fun Day Fairies," said King Oberon. "Megan the Monday Fairy, Tara the Tuesday Fairy, Willow the Wednesday Fairy, Thea the Thursday Fairy, Felicity the Friday Fairy, Sienna the Saturday Fairy, and Sarah the Sunday Fairy."

The fairies managed to smile at Rachel and Kirsty, but they still looked sad. The girls felt sorry for them.

"How do the Fun Day Flags work?" asked Kirsty.

"Come with us to the golden pool," Queen Titania replied, "and we'll show you."

The queen led the way through the palace gardens to the magic pool. They all clustered around as the queen waved her wand over the pool. Immediately, the water began to shimmer with fairy magic.

"Today Francis, the Royal Time Guard, went to the Book of Days to check which day it was. He does that every morning," Queen Titania said, pointing at the pool. "The Book of Days is kept in the Time Tower, on the other side of the place gardens."

Rachel and Kirsty watched as a gleaming white marble tower appeared on the surface of the pool. The tower had a golden flagpole on top, and a beautiful grassy courtyard full of orange and lemon trees to one side. In the middle of the grassy courtyard was a giant clock. It was made of dazzling white and gold tiles. The girls saw Francis hop inside the tower and over to a large, leather-bound book sitting on a rainbow-colored pedestal.

"That's the Book of Days," the queen explained. "It keeps track of the days of the week in case Francis forgets."

As Rachel and Kirsty watched, Francis left the book and went over to a golden cabinet on one side of the room. He took out some bright red material and unfolded it.

"It's a flag," Rachel said.

"It's beautiful!" added Kirsty.

The flag was big and rectangular, with a large sun surrounded by rays of light in the middle. The sun was the same color as the rest of the flag, but it was made of a sparkling fabric. It glittered in the sunlight streaming in through the windows of the Time Tower.

"That's my Monday Fun Flag," said a sad voice.

Rachel and Kirsty glanced at Megan the Monday Fairy. She wore a purpley-blue dress with a red sash. Her long, glossy black hair was held back by a red headband. She looked like she should be laughing and having fun, but instead her face was sad.

In the image in the pool, Francis had now climbed to the top of the Time Tower and was attaching the Monday Fun Flag to the flagpole.

"Do you see Megan waiting down in the courtyard?" asked Queen Titania as the picture changed. Megan was standing in the middle of the tiled clock, at the spot where the two hands met. She had her wand in one hand and was gazing up at the flag.

"When the sun's rays reflect off the shiny parts of the flag, magical sparkles stream down to where Megan is waiting," Queen Titania explained. "This is how the Fun Day Fairies recharge their wands and make sure that they have enough magic for their special day of the week."

"It takes a lot of magic to make sure humans can have fun for a whole day!" Megan added.

Kirsty and Rachel watched as Francis raised the flag to the top of the flagpole. Down in the courtyard, Megan held up her wand.

But just as the sunshine was about to hit
the flag, there was a sudden gust of wind.

Rachel and Kirsty gasped. Jack Frost was whizzing toward the flagpole on the blast of air. He snatched the Monday Fun Flag from the flagpole and zoomed away, cackling!

A Clever Clue

"Oh no!" Rachel cried.

"Poor Megan," said Kirsty, putting her arm around the fairy.

"That's not all." Megan sighed, pointing to the pool. "Look. . . ."

As Francis hurried down from the flagpole, some of Jack Frost's goblins appeared and dashed inside the tower.

They quickly pulled open the golden
cabinet where the Fun Day Flags
were kept.

"Let's take *all* the Fun Day Flags!"
shouted one.

"Yes, then we can have fun all the
time," another yelled gleefully. "And
nobody else can!"

The goblins began grabbing the flags
from the golden cabinet.

"Stop!" Francis shouted, hopping through the doorway. He tried to pull one of the flags away from the nearest goblin. "Give those back!"

"No way!" the goblins cried. They rushed for the door, whooping loudly and waving the flags. Poor Francis was pushed aside as they charged out of the Time Tower.

"Poor Francis!" Rachel exclaimed, as

the pictures in the pool began to fade. "The goblins stole all the flags!"

Queen Titania nodded. "But Jack Frost doesn't have them anymore," she said with a smile. "Watch what happened. . . ." She waved her wand over the pool again.

Rachel and Kirsty watched as a new picture appeared. It showed Jack Frost's ice castle. Three goblins were sliding down the frozen banisters of

the staircase, squealing with delight. Four goblins were playing hide-and-seek. One of them peeked out from behind Jack Frost's ice throne. Other goblins were playing soccer with a solid ball of ice. Some were even skating on the icy floor of the throne room, doing twists and turns and jumps. "The goblins are having fun!" Kirsty laughed.

"That's the power of the Fun Day Flags," explained Megan.

Now the picture changed again to show Jack Frost stomping angrily down the hallway toward his bedroom. "Will you stop having fun and get back to work?" he shouted at his goblins.

Rachel and Kirsty's eyes widened as Jack Frost opened the bedroom door. A stream of warm water cascaded over him from above.

"Help!" Jack Frost yelled, jumping around in a fury. "I'm soaked!"

A second later, a bucket tumbled down from the top of the door. It fell over his head, muffling his voice. Rachel and Kirsty laughed. Meanwhile, the goblins who had set up the trick were peeking around the corner, giggling loudly.

"That's it!" Jack Frost roared, yanking the bucket off his head. "I'm fed up with all this fun!"

He raised his wand and shouted a spell.
"Goblins have no time for fun, so Fun
Day Flags, you must be gone!"

Immediately, a fierce wind whirled
through the ice palace. While the goblins
watched in dismay, it whisked the flags
out the window.

"So where are the flags now?" asked
Rachel, as the pictures faded.

"Jack Frost's spell carried them into the human world, where they became bigger," replied Queen Titania. "But the goblins missed the fun they were having, so some of them snuck off to look for the flags."

"That's why we have to go find the flags before they do," added Megan. "Will you help, girls?"

"Of course we will," said Kirsty.

"Where should we start?" asked Rachel.

Francis stepped forward. He took out his pocket watch and opened the lid. Immediately, a cloud of magic sparkles swirled out of the watch, and the Book of Days appeared in his hands.

"I think there might be a clue in the Book of Days," he croaked, showing one of the pages to Megan, Rachel, and Kirsty. "Look, instead of saying what day it is, now there's a poem on the Monday page."

Kirsty read the poem aloud:

"Searching near and searching far,
I know where the Fun Day Flags are.
Look for Monday with the shoes.
Tip and tap are your two clues."

"If we figure out what the poem means, we'll find the flag!" said Rachel excitedly.

"Tip and tap . . ." Kirsty repeated thoughtfully. "I wonder what that could mean."

Everyone frowned, thinking hard.

Then, suddenly, Rachel gasped. "Oh!" she said, her eyes shining. "I've got it!"

Finding the Flag

Everyone turned, looking eagerly at Rachel.

"Tip and tap!" Rachel said excitedly. "Kirsty, what does that remind you of?"

Kirsty looked confused.

"Remember this morning?" Rachel went on.

Suddenly Kirsty's face lit up. "You mean Karen and her tap dancing lesson!" she cried. "Do you think the Monday flag might  be with Karen's new tap shoes?"

Rachel nodded and quickly explained to the fairies and Francis what Kirsty meant. "Karen's lesson is at the town hall this afternoon," she added. "We'd better get there right away!"

"I'll send you there with magic," said Queen Titania, raising her wand.

"I'll come, too," Megan announced. "I may not have my Fun Day magic, but I might be able to help with my normal fairy magic!"

The two girls closed their eyes as Queen Titania showered them with golden fairy dust.

"Good luck!" the other fairies called.

A moment later, Kirsty and Rachel could hear the sound of traffic. They opened their eyes to find themselves next to Tippington Town Hall.

"Where's Megan?" asked Rachel.

"Here I am!" called Megan, popping out from behind a nearby mailbox. She fluttered over to Kirsty's shoulder, hiding herself behind Kirsty's hair.

"There's Karen," Rachel said suddenly, pointing at the town hall steps.

Karen looked miserable. She was sitting on the steps with her chin in her hands.

"Hi, Karen," called Rachel. "What's wrong?"

"Oh, Rachel," Karen gulped. "Mom dropped me off a little early for my class, so I put my bag down while I was practicing some steps. But when I turned around, my bag was gone!"

"Were your new shoes in the bag?" asked Kirsty.

Karen nodded, biting her lip.

"Oh, I wish I could help Karen have fun," Megan whispered in Kirsty's ear, "but I can't do that without my Fun Day magic."

"Here comes my dance teacher, Miss
Henry," Karen said tearfully. "I don't
want to miss my class."

"Karen, what's the matter?" asked Miss
Henry, when she saw Karen's sad face.

Karen quickly explained.

"I can lend you a pair of tap shoes for
today, so you won't miss class," Miss
Henry said kindly. "And afterward, I'll
help you find your bag."

"And Kirsty and I will look for it while you have your lesson," Rachel added.

"Thanks," Karen said, looking more cheerful as she followed her teacher into the town hall.

Rachel turned to Kirsty and Megan. "Let's start by looking around here," she suggested.

But Kirsty was frowning. "I can hear a strange noise," she whispered.

"So can I," Megan agreed. "It sounds like someone muttering."

Rachel listened, too. "It's coming from around the side of the building," she said.

Megan and the girls went over to the corner and peeked around.

"It's a goblin!" Kirsty whispered.

"And look what he's holding!" added Rachel.

The goblin was poking around inside a blue bag. As Megan and the girls watched, he began trying to pull a piece of shiny red material from it.

"That's my flag!" Megan cried.

The goblin got more and more annoyed because the flag would not come out. Suddenly, he looked up and saw the girls and Megan watching him. With an angry shriek, he grabbed the bag and ran away.

Clock-Watching

"Get him!" Megan cried, zooming off after the goblin.

Rachel and Kirsty followed her on foot. Up ahead, the goblin whizzed around the corner and out of sight.

"He's gone around the back of the hall," Kirsty panted.

"That's where the Clock Tower is," Rachel puffed, pointing.

When the girls and Megan reached the corner, they were just in time to see the goblin dash through the big wooden door at the bottom of the Clock Tower. As they rushed over, the goblin slammed the door shut.

"He locked it from the inside!" Kirsty exclaimed, pulling on the handle.

Rachel put her ear to the door. "I think he's going up the stairs," she reported.

"Let's fly to the top and see what he's up to," said Megan, lifting her wand. With a shower of sparkling fairy dust, Megan turned the girls into fairies. Then they flew to the top of the Clock Tower.

There, the three friends could hear the goblin chuckling with glee behind the large white clock face.

"Look," Megan said, pointing at the clock. The minute hand was bouncing up and down. "The goblin's having fun because of my Monday Fun Flag!"

The girls could hear the goblin laughing as he played with the gears controlling the clock's hands. Rachel, Kirsty, and Megan zipped around the Clock Tower, looking for a way in. But they couldn't find one! "It's no use. There's no way in." Kirsty sighed.

"Then we'll just have to get the goblin out!" said Rachel firmly.

"How?" asked Megan.

They all thought hard.

Suddenly, Rachel had an idea. "The clock chimes every hour," she said. "And it's really loud. It must be even louder inside, near the bells. I bet all that noise will drive the goblin out!"

"But it's only ten-fifteen," Kirsty pointed out.

"I could use my magic to make the chimes ring," Megan said eagerly.

She sent a stream of fairy dust toward the clock. Immediately, the hands began to zoom around toward the eleven o'clock position.

Bong!

The bells began to chime. They were so loud that Megan, Rachel, and Kirsty quickly flew back to the ground to escape the noise.

Bong!

"The goblin won't be able to stand it!" Kirsty laughed as Megan waved her wand and turned Rachel and Kirsty back to their usual size.

Bong!

Suddenly, the door of the Clock Tower flew open. The goblin rushed out, groaning loudly. He was trying to hang on to Karen's bag and cover his ears at the same time, but the bag kept slipping from his grasp.

Kirsty stepped forward and caught it as it fell. "Thank you," she said politely.

The goblin didn't seem to care. "This is no fun at all!" he wailed. Clapping his hands firmly over his ears, he dashed off.

"Look!" Megan said, hovering above the bag, beaming. She pointed her wand at one of the side pockets. A sparkling piece of red material was poking out. "Girls, it's my Monday Fun Flag!"

Time for Fun

Rachel and Kirsty smiled at each other.

"Let's go give Karen her bag," Rachel said, tucking the flag safely under her arm.

Kirsty and Megan nodded eagerly.

"And then I'll bring the Monday flag back to Fairyland, where it belongs," Megan said.

They went into the town hall together,

with Megan perched on Kirsty's shoulder.
The girls followed the sound of music
coming from a room at the back of
the building. They peered through the
window in the door.

Karen was in the
middle of a group of
girls tip-tapping their
way across the room.
Miss Henry watched,
shaking her head and
frowning. Karen and the
other girls didn't look very happy, either.

"We'll try that again," Miss Henry
said, stopping the music. "You all seem
to have forgotten the steps."

One girl sighed loudly. "I just can't get
them right," she said.

"Neither can I," added another.

"No one's having any fun," Megan whispered to Kirsty. "And I can't help until I've recharged my wand with Monday magic!"

Suddenly, Karen noticed Rachel and Kirsty at the door. A big smile lit up her face when she saw the bag in Kirsty's hand. She dashed over and flung the door open. "Thank you! Where was it?" she asked.

"Around the side of the town hall," Rachel told her.

"How did it get there?" Karen asked. Luckily, she didn't wait for an answer. She was too busy pulling the bag open and taking out her sparkly new tap shoes.

"They're beautiful!" Kirsty said, as
Karen quickly took off her
borrowed shoes and put
on the new ones.

"Maybe I'll dance
better now," Karen
said, smiling. "I can't
seem to get any of the
steps right today!" She waved at the girls
as she hurried back to join the class.
"Thanks so much!"

"I must get back to Fairyland to
recharge my wand," Megan said
urgently. "Do you want to come?"

The girls nodded and Megan lifted her
wand. In a shower of magic fairy dust,
they were all whisked away to Fairyland.

King Oberon, Queen Titania, Francis,
and the Fun Day Fairies were waiting

outside the Time Tower. They all cheered as Megan, Rachel, and Kirsty appeared with the Monday flag.

"Great job!" called King Oberon happily. "Francis, please fly the flag!"

Francis took the flag from Rachel and rushed inside the Time Tower.

Meanwhile, Megan zoomed over to the tiled clock in the middle of the courtyard and stood at the spot where the hands met. She raised her wand high and waited.

Rachel and Kirsty held their breath while they watched Francis raise the Monday Fun Flag to the top of the flagpole. As it reached the top, golden rays of sun

struck the flag. Rachel and Kirsty gasped as a beam of dazzling sunlight was reflected down into the courtyard toward Megan. The golden light hit the tip of Megan's wand, which immediately sparkled with a magical red glow. Everyone clapped and cheered.

"Hooray!" Megan cried, dancing with joy. "Now I can put the fun back into Monday!"

Rachel and Kirsty rushed to join her.

"Thank you, girls!" called Queen Titania as everyone shouted goodbye.

Megan lifted her wand and, in a sparkling flash, whisked herself and the girls back to the hallway outside Karen's dance class. Peeking through the window, they saw one girl accidentally bump into Karen and nearly send her flying. Everyone still looked sad.

"Time for some Monday fun!" Megan whispered.

Rachel and Kirsty watched as the little fairy poked the tip of her wand through the keyhole in the door. A stream of red sparkles drifted into the room and swirled around the dancers, but they were all too busy concentrating on their steps to notice.

"Stop, girls!" called Miss Henry
suddenly, switching off the CD player
with a smile. "I have an idea!" She went
over to a closet and dragged out a large
cardboard box. "I was going to save
these for later, but I think it would be fun
to use them now. . . ."

"That's because of my Fun Day magic!"
Megan whispered to Rachel and Kirsty.

The box was full of feather boas, shiny
canes, and glittery top hats.
The dancers looked
very excited as
they pulled them
out of the box.
Rachel and Kirsty
grinned as they saw

how thrilled Karen was to find a sparkly
top hat the same color as her new tap

shoes. She also chose a fluffy purple boa
and a shiny black cane.

"Now, girls," called Miss Henry,
beaming as she put a toe-tapping tune
on the CD player, "let's try these new
steps. Follow me!"

Rachel, Kirsty, and Megan watched as
the teacher began tip-tapping her way
around the room, twirling her
cane. The dancers did the
same, laughing as they tried
to follow her. But this time,
even though the steps
were more
complicated, they all
did much better.

"Everyone's having fun!"
Rachel declared, happy to
see Karen's smiling face.

"Yes, I'm so glad!" Megan replied, grinning. "Thank you, girls." She lifted her wand and waved at Rachel and Kirsty. "Now I have to go catch up on my Monday Fun Day work!"

The girls nodded.

"Good-bye, Megan!" Rachel called.

"We'll keep looking for the other Fun Day Flags!" Kirsty promised. The little fairy blew them a kiss and zoomed away.

Rachel and Kirsty took one last look at the happy faces in the tap dancing class, grinned at each other, and then headed home.

THE FUN DAY FAIRIES

Megan the Monday Fairy has
her flag back. Now Rachel
and Kirsty must help

Tara
the Tuesday
Fairy!

Field Day Sparkle

"Come on, Rachel! You can do it!"
Kirsty Tate cheered as she watched her
friend sprint down the sunny field. Today
was Tippington Schools' Field Day. The
three local schools had come together to
compete in all sorts of different games
and sports. Kirsty was staying with her
best friend, Rachel Walker, in

Tippington during school break, so she had come along to watch.

The 100-yard dash was the last race of the morning, and Rachel was doing really well.

"Come on, Rachel, keep going!" Kirsty yelled. The two runners were so close, it was impossible to guess who was going to win. At the very last moment, Rachel surged past the other girl and crossed the finish line first.

"Yay! Rachel wins!" Kirsty cheered, jumping up and down. She beamed at some of the other children who had watched the race, but they all looked unhappy. *They must have wanted the other girl to win really badly,* Kirsty thought.

Rachel came over a few moments later,

smiling. Her face was flushed. "Phew —
that was a close one," she panted.

Kirsty smiled. "What an exciting race!"

"Well, I thought so," Rachel said. "But
have you noticed that everyone else
seems really bored?"

Kirsty looked around. It was true. A
girl nearby was scuffing the grass with
her foot and complaining to her dad that
she was too cold. One of the older boys
was saying that he was hungry. Even
some of the teachers seemed bored.

A startling thought struck both girls at
exactly the same time. "It must be
because the Tuesday Fun Flag is
missing," Kirsty said in a low voice.

"That's just what I was about to say,"
Rachel agreed. "That explains why
nobody is having fun today!"

Come flutter by Butterfly Meadow!

Butterfly Meadow #1: Dazzle's First Day
Dazzle is a new butterfly, fresh out of her cocoon. She doesn't know how to fly, and she's all alone! But Butterfly Meadow could be just what Dazzle is looking for.

Butterfly Meadow #2: Twinkle Dives In
Twinkle is feisty, fun, and always up for an adventure. But the nearby pond holds much more excitement than she expected!